THE MELLOPS STRIKE OIL

by Tomi Ungerer

Φ

Phaidon Press Limited
Regent's Wharf
All Saints Street
London, N1 9PA

Phaidon Press Inc.
180 Varick Street
New York, NY 10014

www.phaidon.com

This edition © 2011 Phaidon Press Limited
First published in German as
Familie Mellops findet Öl by Diogenes
© 1978 Diogenes Verlag AG Zürich

ISBN 978 0 7148 6249 1
002-0711

A CIP catalogue record for this book is available
from the British Library.

Printed in China

One summer morning Mr. Mellops, his sons, and their dog went cycling through the countryside.

At lunchtime they found a nice shady spot
for a picnic. Mr. Mellops laid out all the
food. "But we have nothing to drink!"
Ferdinand complained.

"Don't worry! There's fresh water over there,"
Casimir said, pointing to a brook. He went
to fetch water for everyone.

"Pfff! That water is awful. It tastes like oil!" Father said. "Hmm, I wonder whether oil is under the ground nearby. Oil is worth a fortune! This could turn into a very prosperous picnic!"

Mr. Mellops and the dog hurried back to town.
At the public library he gathered books about
how to find oil.

Father's books said that oil was found in areas with lots of fossils, especially ones called ammonites, belemnites and ceriths. The boys explored the brook and found all kinds of stones and fossils! But were they the right kind?

They took them to the museum to have them identified.

They discovered that these objects were:

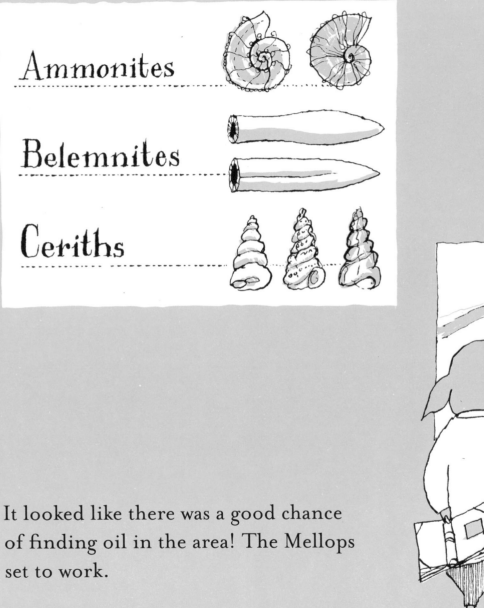

Ammonites

Belemnites

Ceriths

It looked like there was a good chance of finding oil in the area! The Mellops set to work.

Back at the brook, they hastily built a wooden
tower, called a derrick, which would make
it easier for them to drill into the ground
to reach the oil.

Mr. Mellops fixed a mechanical drilling device of his own invention to the top of the derrick. And then they started to drill.

The drilling took a long time, so the boys
decided to set up camp.

Father's system was powered by the wind, like
a Dutch windmill. The boys pumped water from
the brook to soften the ground for the drill.

When there was no wind the Mellops relaxed
and had a good time.

Isidor ran around chasing butterflies.

Mrs. Mellops joined her family
and made a campfire to cook on.

In the evening the owls came to listen
to Mr. and Mrs. Mellops' duet.

The next morning, the Mellops built an oil tank. This is where they would keep the oil when they found it.

Later that day the ground beneath them began
to shake and suddenly, a fountain of oil spurted
from a hole where they had been drilling.
"We've struck oil!" they cried.

The poor dog was caught in the jet of oil.
He howled with fright.

To save him the Mellops decided to stop the
jet of oil by covering the hole with the tank.

They had to work quickly. Casimir and
Felix cut down trees while Isidor and
Ferdinand created a makeshift path over
which they could move the tank.

Then, by rolling the tank over the logs,
they placed it over the flow of oil.

The plan worked perfectly... until the dog
landed on Mr. Mellops' head!

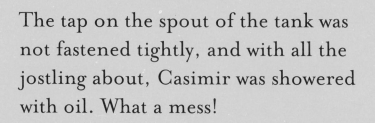

The tap on the spout of the tank was not fastened tightly, and with all the jostling about, Casimir was showered with oil. What a mess!

Meanwhile, on a road nearby, a passerby threw
away a burning cigar. It smouldered on some
dry twigs, and then caught fire.

The Mellops were soon surrounded
by flames. The oil was sure to catch light
and explode! Mr. Mellops pierced holes in the hose,
and his sons pulled it around the oil tank. Then
they pumped water through the hose and drenched
the ground to stop the fire getting close to the oil.

Suddenly Mr. Mellops exclaimed, "Where is Mrs. Mellops?" The family ran to look for her.

Back at the campsite Mrs. Mellops was
trapped in the flames! The fire was hot
on her heels.

Thank goodness! She made it to the river just in time where the flames couldn't reach her.

When the fire had passed the Mellops were reunited.
Together, they trudged home through the charred
forest. "Oil drilling is quite exciting," Father sighed.
"But from now on, let's leave it to the professionals."

When they arrived home they took hot baths to remove the oil and ashes.

Clean and dry once again, the Mellops sat in their garden and had dinner. "What an adventurous picnic!" said Casimir. "Yes," agreed Father, "but I think I've had enough adventure for some time. I'd rather be here with you all, eating delicious cream cake!"